First published in the United States, Great Britain, Canada, Australia, and New Zealand
in 2011 by NorthSouth Book, Inc., an imprint of NordSüd Verlag AG, CH-8005 Zürich,
Switzerland. First hardcover edition published in 2014.

Distributed in the United States by NorthSouth Books, Inc., New York 10016.
Library of Congress Cataloging-in-Publication Data is available.
Printed in Germany by Grafisches Centrum Cuno GmbH & Co. KG,
Calbe, April 2014

ISBN: 978-0-7358-4188-8 (trade)

1 3 5 7 9 • 10 8 6 4 2

www.northsouth.com

FSC
www.fsc.org
MIX
Paper from
responsible sources
FSC® C043106

Owl Howl

Paul Friester ◈ Philippe Goossens

North South

One afternoon in the forest, the air was filled with a terrible howl. "*HOO . . . HOO . . .*" At first, the animals thought it was the old wolf.

The hedgehog was the first to investigate.
With all his prickles, he felt very brave. He
crept cautiously to the big tree.

It wasn't the wolf! It was a tiny owl.
She was howling miserably.

"What's wrong?" asked the hedgehog.
"Did you fall out of your nest?"

But the little owl just shook her head
and kept on howling.

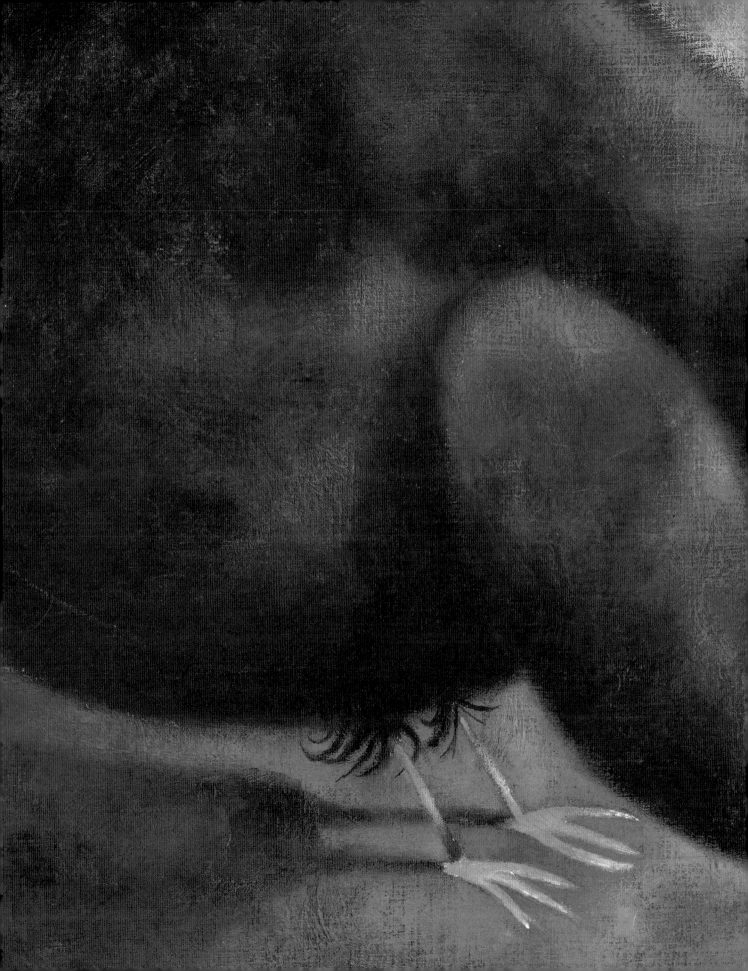

Next the crow swooped down.
"Do you want to play?"
he asked the owl.
But the little owl just shook
her head and kept on howling.

Suddenly there was a rustling in the bushes.
"Are you hungry?" asked the squirrel,
bursting with curiosity. "I have a nut for you."
But the little owl didn't want a nut
and just kept on howling.

"What is going on here?" asked the mole.
And he said to the little owl, "If you stop
howling, I will give you something nice."

The mole dug his way to the meadow
and came back with a colorful necklace
made of flowers.

But the little owl just shook her head
and kept on howling.

The old stag beetle scuttled along next. He looked at the owl sternly.

"You should be ashamed of yourself, howling like that. This sort of thing never happened in my day. I'm going to nip your bottom."

Now the little owl howled even louder.

"Look what you have done," scolded the animals.

The stag beetle felt terrible and ran to find a large cobweb.

"Why don't we rock the little owl?" he suggested. "She is sure to like that."

So they rocked the little owl. The mole
even hummed a lullaby.
    But the little owl just kept on howling.
    Then suddenly she flew right out of
the hammock . . .

. . . and straight into the wings of
Mommy Owl.

"What's wrong, sweetheart? Why are
you howling like that?" asked Mommy Owl.

All the animals held their breath, waiting
to hear the answer.

The little owl stopped howling at once.
She sniffed a little and then cheeped quietly:

"I forgot."

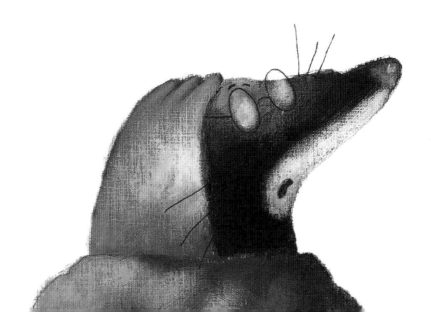